Lazy Fascist Press
Portland, Oregon
PO Box 10065
Portland, OR 97296

www.lazyfascistpress.com
lazyfascist@gmail.com

ISBN: 978-1-62105-146-6

Cover Design by Matthew Revert
www.matthewrevert.com

Edited by Cameron Pierce

Printed in the USA.

THE LAST HORROR NOVEL IN THE HISTORY OF THE WORLD

Brian Allen Carr

WELCOME TO THE LAST HORROR NOVEL:
AN INTRODUCTION BY TOM WILLIAMS

The Mexico/Texas border—near which Brian Allen Carr has lived most of his writing life—is easily demarcated on a map. The Rio Grande separates the nation and the state (though, as its ad agencies would like us to remember, Texas is "a whole other country"), yet it can be an easily traversed border, and the influences that flow back and forth cannot be overlooked, as it's easy to wander through the streets of, say, Nuevo Laredo and think things look much like a typical US city, or stumble upon a section of McAllen and think it would fit right into Mexico. In all, if borders are meant to designate two different sides, the Rio Grande is doing a pretty lousy job.

To be true, the border that exists between fiction deemed as literary and that deemed as genre is far better policed and regulated than that between Mexico and Texas. I would go so far as to venture to say that the natives on each side are far more hostile toward one another, and that as soon as one has crossed over, she need not attempt to return. Further, unlike the somewhat naturally occurring Rio Grande as border, the divide between literary and genre is entirely manmade and likely as unnecessary as, a Texan might say, tits on a teacup.

Yet there it lies, forcing literary writers to gripe about vampire teen detective novels (while whispering about their "guilty pleasures" of fantasy, sci-fi, thriller, or English cozy) and ginning up the defensiveness of genre writers who know that pointing to their sales only confirms that something must be wrong on that side of the border, if so many people want to buy those quote unquote books.

And then there is Brian Allen Carr. Like the Texan that he is, who daily breathes air scented by both cultures while digging into a hybrid cuisine, he moves easily across borders. None of the jabs the natives of literary and genre fiction might fling at him can penetrate his defense. His sentences soar, his action entices. His sharks scare more than Spielberg's, while his characterizations help you know every-damn-body in the book as well as a best friend. And in this ineffable novella—part-apocalypse narrative, part-fable, part-prayer—he rains down terror so indescribable you have to read it for yourself while breaking your heart when his characters share their secrets.

In this fantastic (in both senses of the word) fiction, Brian Allen Carr reminds us that borders are not to be feared but forded, crisscrossed and zigzagged until no border remains and a new frontier results. What we need after *The Last Horror Novel in the History of the World* is a modifier to describe his accomplishment. Carresque? Carrvian? I'm going with Carrful. Because that's where I want to be with Brian Allen Carr: riding in the backseat with his indelible prose, unerring comedy, mad scientist plot, and social worker heart while he howls behind the wheel, foot on the accelerator, ninety-miles an hour, headed for the abyss.

THE LAST HORROR NOVEL
IN THE HISTORY OF
THE WORLD

the dissolves

Scrape, Texas—far from fame or infamy—appeared on maps, was passed through by travelers. A blink of crummy buildings, wooden households—the harsh-hearted look of them, like a thing that's born old.

When we stood on the rooftop of Blue Parson's tree house, we could see, in the navy, swollen night sky, the orange glow of better towns to be from, could hear the highways to them hissing with car traffic and train horns cooing from their age-rusted tracks. We knew the direction, you just didn't see us walking. The salt smell of the bayside was the church of our childhood, and we would not play the role of heretic just because America said, in its school-mannered way, "If you stay where you come from, you're doomed to repeat yourself."

What we sadly witnessed, what fate befell us, never happened to anyone in this whole world's history.

But, tragically, will never happen again.

The black magic of bad living only looks hideous to honest eyes.

These few streets at dusk, still except for tarrying dogs, their milk-heavy tits swaying.

Rob Cooder breaks a banjo string, clears his throat, smokes cloves.

Mindy Stuart has herpes.

Tim Bittles has a cell phone and is on it, texting a girl named Meredith two towns over, and every time she obliges with a picture, he shows us her faceless nudity on the screen.

Scarlett and Teddy are in love, say: we'll quit Scrape, Texas when we can. Put everything of worth into a U-Haul, drive to Austin and get schooling in us and not look back ever.

"Good. Good. Do it. You should."

Scrape lies between two legitimate cities.

Corpus Christi and Houston.

There are saltwater puddles the whole way between them.

There's the constant smell of turning fish.

On the water, boats with filled sails slow their patterns eternal.

We pull crab traps from the shallows, cast dead shrimp at unseen trout, gig flounder in the nighttime, shoot Redhead drake from bleak-winter skies.

We invent a game to anger the city folk.

Rob and Tim go to the highway and drive thirty-five miles an hour side by side.

There's no way to pass, so the cars clump up in their commuting.

A line of them stretches back through the night like a string of honking Christmas lights.

Fridays we fry fish in the front yard, the smell of cornmeal caramelizing in the grease.

The mothers make mayonnaise from scratch, mince home-pickled cucumbers for the tartar sauce.

We sing these old songs in the sweater-heavy nighttime air. The glow of streetlights soft in the salt stench.

If I could live my life all over . . .

And Mindy Stuart stares out at nothing over that line, and we all know someone will love her no matter what because the way she looks, and we all know that it won't be the love she craves, because Mindy never likes what she has.

We overdo it, drink until our blood is rust and the prickly sun pinks the sky to dawn.

No one's ready for sleep. We take the john boat down to the laguna and row out to the duck blinds where we hide in the humid morning with shotguns between our legs.

We pass out before the ducks show, wake swollen with mosquito stings.

"What now?" someone asks.

"Let's get drunk again."

We have whiskey and we work on it, toss out decoys and wade the water, dragging our feet to scare away stingrays.

Someone shoots at the sky and we wait a moment.

After a while, birdshot rains down.

"There's so many ripples," someone says. "So many ripples," as the shots land, dimpling the water's surface.

Mindy keeps her herpes secret, crawls in and out of apartments that smell of new carpet and microwaved soup.

She knows the boys of high school intimate.

They are shark-skin smooth and firecracker quick.

They whip in and out of her like snake tongues tasting air.

She examines their tightness, the curls in their hair.

Gives them more than they want of her.

Makes them say her name.

First we saw birds and rabbits, squirrels and frogs, raccoons and possums, crossing through the daytime streets.

"Something's off," Old Burt says. He's racist toward blacks and hates the internet. "It just makes everyone act blacker," he says.

Manny is Mexican and Tyler's black as they come.

Manny says, "You like me?"

"Hell yeah I do," Old Burt says. "We stole this land from your people."

Tyler says, "You like me?"

Old Burt says, "I'm trying, son. I know it's not right. I was trained this way. Imagine how long it took for folks to admit the world wasn't flat." He shakes his head, "But, boy, I just look at you and think the word nigger."

Old Burt loves his guns. He takes the plug out of a twenty gauge pump, walks into his front yard and starts shooting the possums that wander awkwardly in the light, baring their needly teeth when they scare.

He blasts a few to muck, their bodies shredding open with the shots, skidding down into the dirt where swell hunks of them disappear.

"I tell you," Old Burt says, "something ain't right."

14

Newscasts show static.

Mindy lies still in a strange boy's bed. She has a necklace charm that she drags on the chain. It hisses as a zipper might, makes a sort of music in the otherwise silence. She eyes the TV oddly. She drops the charm on her chest, elbows the boy who rests beside her. "Something's wrong with your cable," she says.

The boy rolls away from her. "So fucking sleep," he says.

Tim Bittles sits in the dark cabin of his Ford truck, his face aglow with his cell phone's light. He nods at it, then unzips his pants. He takes his dick firm in his grip, the erect length of it swelling, the faint smell of sweat and sweet. He presses a button on his phone and a bright light flashes, taking a pale picture. "This what u like," he types, then hits send.

He waits.

He waits for a reply.

For a long time he waits, but nothing.

He shrugs, shakes his head, and keys the ignition.

The starter hacks electric, and the engine turns over.

Tim Bittles puts his dick away.

Tim Bittles drives into the night.

Blue Parson stands on his rooftop. Rob Cooder sits Indian style picking banjo notes.

Suddenly, the distant city lights go dim.

"See that?" asks Blue.

"What?" asks Rob.

"The lights?"

"What about 'em."

"They're gone."

Rob stands beside Blue, both dumbfounded.

"Power outage, you reckon?" Rob asks.

"Maybe," says Blue, "let's check the news."

Rob climbs down the tree house ladder, Blue takes the zip line. They cross the yard, enter Blue's home. The TV, which stays permanently on, says, "No signal."

Teddy sets a box in the back of the U-Haul.

"I think that's it," Scarlett tells him.

Teddy smiles, nods, then jumps for the handle, hangs from it as the cargo door lowers. "Sure you don't want to leave tonight?" he asks.

"Sure," Scarlett says. "I've already rolled out the sleeping bag."

The two hug, kiss.

Scarlett pulls Teddy by the hand and leads him back into their garage apartment.

Tessa says, "Cash only," when Blue sets the Lone Star sixer on the counter.

"Who the hell carries cash?"

"No one," Tessa says, smiles. "But the machine ain't working."

"Like, ain't reading the cards? Like, you tried that plastic bag trick?"

"Shit," says Tessa, "it ain't the plastic bag trick." Her dyed-blonde hair is tightly braided into ropes pulled back into a ponytail of coils. "Thing ain't connecting."

"Shit," says Blue. "I ain't got cash."

"Sucks to be you," says Tessa.

Blue frowns, shrugs. "C'mon," he says, "lemme pay you tomorrow." He smiles all his charm at her.

Tessa takes a blonde braid in her hand, twirls it around a finger. "Blue, you ain't trustworthy."

"Is that a yes?"

Tessa shakes her head. She looks at the camera on the ceiling. She knows it doesn't work. "Shit," she says, "long as you promise."

Blue smiles. "In that case," he says, "I'm gonna switch this out for a twelve."

Manny flinches each time Old Burt pulls the trigger. Tyler twists a blunt as bits of raccoon and rat fleck his sneakers. Burt fires again at the roving critters, says, "What could be causing it?"

Tyler lights up. "Who fucking knows?" Tyler says. "Want some of this?" he asks, tries to pass to Old Burt. The smell of bud and gunpowder stinks up the air.

Old Burt shakes his head, "You know I can't smoke after you," he says. "Pass it to Manny first."

Tyler shakes his head. "You'll smoke after him?"

Old Burt shrugs. "I'm sorry," he says, "he's just closer my kind." Old Burt blasts an armadillo and chambers another shell. "You don't gotta make me feel guilty about it."

Tyler grits his teeth. "I don't know why the fuck I hang out with you," he says and passes Manny the blunt.

"Thanks," says Manny, and he fills his lungs with smoke, passes back to Tyler, exhales toward the sky, thick with all manner of birds flying toward the gulf.

"Hey," says Burt. "It was my turn."

Tyler hits it, says, "Nope," as he chokes the smoke down. He holds the blunt at Burt. "It's your turn now."

Old Burt contemplates the blunt. He looks at Tyler, he

looks at Manny, he looks at Tyler again. "Fine," says Old Burt, "but don't go telling no one you saw me do it." He takes the blunt in his fingers.

Tessa says, "Cash only, credit card machine's down."

"I ain't got no fucking credit card," Mindy says as she sets her quart on the counter.

Tessa rolls her eyes. "Just the Miller then?"

Mindy shakes her head no, says, "Pack of Camel Crush." She points to the black and blue pack. "What the fuck's wrong with the machine?" she asks. "Ain't nothing working right."

"Don't know," says Tessa as she retrieves the cigarettes, places them on the counter, rings Mindy up. "Just not connecting. Had to spot Blue a twelve pack."

Mindy looks at the camera on the ceiling, flips it the finger, "That thing still broken?" she asks, then, "You know he ain't paying you back."

"Seven fifty," says Tessa, "still broken," she says, "and if he don't pay me back I'll kick his ass. Y'all still fucking?"

Mindy hands Tessa a ten. "Tessa Butcher," she says, "I ain't never fucked no Blue Parson."

Tessa makes change. "Shit," she says, "you fuck everything else."

Mindy stares hard. "Your hair looks like shit," she says.

The two women mad dog each other.

Mindy takes a lighter from a rack on the counter. "I ain't paying for this," she says and leaves the store.

"Can you sleep?" Teddy asks.

"Not hardly," says Scarlett.

"Wanna do something?" Teddy asks.

"Of course I do," says Scarlett.

Blue Parson cracks open another, "Nothing better than free beer," he says.

Rob Cooder nods agreement, sips at his own. "Wonder why everything's down?"

The two sit in lawn chairs beneath the tree house, and Tim Bittles pulls up in his Ford. He gets down. "Got one for me?"

"Sure," says Blue, and he fetches a bottle from the ice chest. "But you gotta show me some them cell phone titties for it."

"Shit," says Tim, "you got yourself a deal."

Scarlett pulls Teddy's hands to her throat, grinds up, down, back, and forth. She is giddy with sex pain. She is slick with their thrusting. Her eyes are closed tight, teeth clenched, mouth forming an agony. Teddy says, "You, you?" and Scarlett says, "Yes, yes." And then they are both lowing moans and pressing as firm into the other as they can muster their muscles to press, their minds lost in that light and music and dizzy and space and breathing.

"My daddy would kill me if he knew I was about to do this," Burt says, and he hands a pistol to Tyler.

Tyler smiles.

"You know how to use it, don't ya?"

Tyler holds the pistol sideways, fires a bullet at a nutria rat, and the dirt near it coughs dust.

Old Burt shakes his head. He reaches out and turns Tyler's wrist so the gun is properly held. "Just cause you're a nigger," says Old Burt, "don't mean you gotta act like one."

Tyler shakes his head. "Why come I don't shoot you?" he asks.

Old Burt raises his shotgun and blasts the rat that Tyler couldn't hit. "Prolly cause you'd miss," he answers. "Now try again. And pretend you're white."

Tyler fires at a possum that thumps dead to the dirt.

"There you go," says Burt. "How'd it feel?"

Tyler nods, smiles.

Then Manny: "I want a fucking gun too."

Then they hear the screaming.

the screaming

It can't be natural. Light bulbs burst in their sockets and birds fall from the sky, shrieking. Old Burt winces in pain. Tessa watches as the glass windows of the storefront crack in threads like webs. Teddy thinks he's fucking Scarlett better than he ever has. Mindy drops her quart of beer on the sidewalk where it explodes. She falls to her knees, plugs her ears with her fingers. Blue, Rob and Tim drop their beers too. Plug their ears too. Burt, Manny and Tyler drop their guns. Cover their heads. The rabbits and possums and armadillos and raccoons and mice and rats and frogs and deer and birds grow crazier, run in circles, blood leaks from their ears. The water at the edges of the bay and laguna begins to shake, bubble, effervesce. First bait fish float to the surface, crabs belly up. Later, small reds, whiting, flounder, mullet. In the sky, the clouds are dispersed concentric, so above Scrape, the moon can be seen full and pale yellow against a circle of black. Light bulbs continue to burst, raining splinters of glass, sparks of light, and with each one destroyed, the sky goes deeper dark, revealing twinkling stars arranged in myriad constellations. The neon signs of Scrape scream open, rain electric colors. In homes, liquor bottles are toppled from their pedestals, perfume bottles drop and rattle on countertops. Aquariums flood open, and tropical fish wriggle on carpets, their gills aching in search of breath, their tails clapping them about. The temperature rises. In the diner, the butter melts in its foil wrap on the tables, and the ice in Blue Parson's cooler thins to water. Every leaf from every tree limb drops, and the helicopter seeds chop their single bladed flight haphazardly. Chicken eggs explode in refrigerators, yolks and whites scrambling with slivers of shell and mingling into muck heaps at random. Crayons go soft in children's hands. In the fields, cows topple, dung beetles creep queerly from manure piles, roll on their backs, kick their legs at nothing. Dogs howl. Cats hiss. Snakes slither into holes, coil up so their heads are tucked beneath the braids of them. Above, the moon seems to be made alive, red and blue veins show on its surface as though it's some clot of newborn flesh, pale from never seeing sunlight, though the light it's reflecting is just that. The contents of the sandbox in the schoolyard is picked up and blown off in a magnificent wind that scrapes paint from the cars it crosses over. Soccer balls and bicycles and baby dolls are wriggled away from their resting places, redeposited at the phenomenon's whims. Countertop fryers dance until they drop on linoleum, spilling their rancid grease in pools that ooze slowly with bits of caramelized flour shimmying in the thickness. Lipsticks melt, pools of maroon and crimson emerge at the base of their black containers. Pianos and guitars and violins and cellos and violas in the orchestra room of the high school emit all their notes in unison. The cooler doors of the convenience store spill open under the weight of the toppled beverages they contain, and Gatorades and Coca-Colas and Pepsis and chocolate milks and Budweisers fumble out into the aisles, the glass containers cracking and rivers of beer and soda flood across the tile floor, down the grout lines. Coins rattle in car ashtrays. Keys jingle where they sit. Books fall from shelves. Coats limp from their hangers in the closets. The pilot lights in all the ovens extinguish. Old ladies lose their wigs, contact lenses. Dentures drop from their mouths. Babies shit themselves. Then the words. Carried on the screams. Thick as cement. "Where are my children?"

There is a legend, and it varies in telling. Some say it's 500 years old, others, less than 100. It centers on this: a woman is left by a man.

Is it Malinche, Cortez's translator and concubine? Is it a peasant who fell in love over lies? Either way, there are children. Most say two, and most say this: The woman is deceived, destroyed, heartbroken.

The man desires the companionship and matrimony of one closer to his station, one of his own race, nationality.

Once content to confine his time with the mother of his children, the lowly status of her lineage grows troublesome to him, and their current proximity to poverty, while once poetic, romantic, intoxicating in its reality, becomes laborious, repulsive, complicated and terrifying.

Could it be catching, the squalor? If you mix yourself into that cocktail of ill-repute, can you come clean of its contents and rise to your rightful spot in society?

First, there is love.

Let's say the couple occupies themselves in the sunshine of the world, clipping flowers that they dry by hanging upside down in front of open windows—the perfume of their drying, soporific and warm.

There is no music, but alas they are dancing.

Draped in quilts of lavender-dyed cotton, the man and woman read fairytales to their children—cautionary things that expound on the positive results of behaving with virtue, dust-flavored stories where witches drown and spoiled princes are punished.

But it's terrifying to turn your back on your training, and in these moments the man is bungled by internal whispers that revoke his current joys and manifest self-doubt.

The man's protocol, preached to him since birth, is this: Find a woman of strong history, pleasing form and well-postured behaviors, woo her, win her, and have her bear you children. Endow these children with your knowledge. Bless them with your name. Gift them with inheritances. And pray that your line endures strong for eternity.

To the woman chosen, this notion is lost. To her, you seek love. She can't conceive the trepidation mounting in her husband's heart every time her family appears dressed in tattered clothing, playing music on botched instruments with broken strings, drinking until they forget their own language.

She is prideful in the strength of her own charms. She believes the warmth of her affections are celestial-sent, predetermined by heavens. In her mind and soul, the matrimony she's engaged in is somehow woven into the fabric of the galaxy and her husband's eyes see beyond her flaws because love allows for every kind of forgiveness.

But, this is far from true.

When alone, wandering amongst his own kind, in the town he never invites his family to from fear of humiliation, he encounters myriad women who embody the stock he knew he was supposed to search for. Often, he curses himself for chancing upon his bride, in a world foreign to him, alive with mystery. It is this mystery he accuses, blaming the unfamiliar surroundings as the catalyst for his faulty feelings. The mother of his children is still pleasing to look at, to hold, but now that the magic of her strangeness has tapered, been undone and made homespun, a nausea at the eternity he's promised her has mounted, made him miserable.

It is not so much a plan he hatches as a notion. He leaves himself open to the suggestion that he might still find his way. After all, their wedding did not occur in his church, under his Lord's eyes, but rather near a river at dusk, the faint wisps of orange sunlight leaking like streaks from the horizon.

"If I am approached," he tells himself, "I will not thwart the advances."

In this way he deceives himself into believing that any engagement that might grow out of his openness would be fatalistic, sent by God, and who would he be to intervene?

Maybe he is sharpening a sword, maybe he is cleaning a rifle, maybe he is checking the mailbox—it all depends on when the story occurred. There is nothing definite beyond this: the man finds a more suitable lover.

On a lark, he meets a woman with money from a respectable family, and, because they are more suited to each other, they fall madly in love, and the man sets his designs on stepping away from his former family and into this new lady's life.

He barely explains this to his wife, says merely, "I'll not be home again," and the wife is heartbroken.

Here the legend becomes murkier, splits in two.

Some say the wife does it immediately, some say years

transpire before it's done.

This is a possibility: the man's new woman cannot bear him children. They try, over and over, they try, but the results are always the same—nothing happens.

The man knows, for his life's plan to be fulfilled, that he must have children to pass his name to. The new wife knows this as well, lays in blankets weeping and watching the sunset, lighting candles and speaking with Jesus.

It is a great internal debate that twists in the man's soul. On the one hand, he already has two children, on the other, they must stay secret or it could be his undoing.

The new wife's depression does not abate. She stays hunkered down in misery, breaking from her woes only long enough to endeavor to conceive again. Each time becomes more wretched—mechanical sex where no one opens their eyes, and afterwards she sits in odd positions that she's discovered in books, because these unique postures are supposed to aid with conception. They do not.

Long is the season of their sadness, and the man schemes a longshot.

He goes to the new wife in her nest of sorrow.

"Do you love me?" he asks.

"More than anything," she tells him.

"Will you always?" he says. "No matter what?"

She becomes curious. "You know I will," she says. "I don't understand?"

"Promise me," the man says. "No matter what."

"I promise," she says, "no matter what," she says, "I always will."

Then comes the confession along with the scheme, "I can go for them," the man says, "I will bring them here," he says, "they will be our children," he tells her, "yours and mine."

Joy glows in the new wife's eyes. "What are you waiting for?" she asks, and the man goes.

Again the legend leaves us to assume. We know nothing of the specifics beyond this—the man travels to his neglected abode. Perhaps, on seeing his return, the old wife goes wild with hope, "Has he returned? Will he stay forever?"

Imagine then the pendulum of her emotion when he professes his purpose, "I've only come for the children."

She breaks in the ache of those words.

Miraculously, she escapes the ex-husband, grabs up her children, flees with one in each arm.

The man gives chase.

Through brush, thorny trees, barbed grasses and crags, he pursues her to the river bank where the two were united in marriage. There, in that horrible hour, darkness of night upon them like a curse, the moon casting shadows with its pale yellow light, the woman decides that if she cannot have her children, no one can.

She looks at them, one last time. At their eyes, confused. Their cheeks tight with fear. Mouths open, panicked breathing. Children perceive everything. How could it turn to this?

Once

upon a time

cradled and sung to

now . . .

They say that drowning does not hurt, but you wouldn't know by the scene.

The woman clinches a handful of hair, from each child, a fist of hair, and buries their faces in the river.

Wild must be the thoughts. Facedown in the water, screaming for Mommy. But Mommy is there. Mommy is holding you. Mommy is holding you down.

Breathe.

Eventually your body makes you.

Breathe.

There is no option.

It thinks it's doing the right thing.

Pulling the brackish water deep in the lungs.

The flavor of river bottom flooding the senses.

Sometimes bad choices keep lasting forever.

the confusion

Mindy's head buzzes in the drone. She staggers, winces, clambers to her feet.

The scream comes again, "Where are my children?" And again the world seems jolted with the wail, and Mindy's on her knees again, her hands hotly scraped on the cement, bleeding.

From behind the counter, Tessa watches Mindy through the cracked window, sees her rise, fall.

The disturbed world shows grainy, and Tessa's ears hiss, echo. She screams for Mindy, but can't hear herself screaming. The sensation is she's lost somehow, but Tessa knows just where she is. Shock hits her, her ribs shake and rattle like she's a kicked dog in fear of being kicked again, and she doesn't want to be alone.

She emerges from behind the counter confusedly, hoping to catch Mindy who has staggered and fallen, risen from the street several times and is now walking with fingers in her ears.

Tessa follows.

Out into the dark of night, shadowed queerly by the transformed moon, she watches Mindy moving forward in a broken gait, her motions staggering.

In the street, debris drifts. Scraps of paper, plastic bags, empty cans scatter on robust winds. Dust is heaved about giving coarse texture to each breath Tessa takes.

Tessa screams, "Mindy," but Tessa can't hear it, Mindy can't hear, or doesn't care to turn.

They continue on, Mindy in the lead, Tessa nearly crying,

trying to catch up but unable to hurry her advance—both girls sort of wandering forward.

"Mindy," Tessa says, "Mindy."

But Mindy stays with fingers buried in ears, only removing them briefly to swipe away bits of magazine pages that blow against her.

"Mindy," Tessa says, and this time she sort of hears it, though her own voice seems far away. "Mindy," again, and now the words are clearer. "Mindy," she calls, and Mindy turns.

Their stares reflect each others' terror. Then, again, loud as destruction, "Where are my children?" And again their sense of sound is muted, hidden, but they go to each other, clutch each other in embrace, cower together in the center of the road.

Tessa sees her first.

A woman in white, her flesh unnatural, and behind her, with her, moving with mirrored steps, multitudes of craggy children dawdle, their countenances suggesting an undeadness, withered things as though plucked from graves, made animate.

Tessa taps Mindy, makes her look, needs to know if she's dropped off into insanity or if others perceive the horror advancing toward her.

And Mindy screams, Tessa can tell by her face, she can't hear it, but she knows Mindy's screaming, so she knows, that which is before her is really there. A kind of army of oddities. Pale figures in disturbed and dated clothing.

And then the woman in white is screaming again. Tessa can't make out the words, but the words are, "Where are my children?"

Old Burt picks up the dropped guns, grabs a few more from a duffle, distributes them to Manny and Tyler, motions them to follow.

The three move through the mess of Scrape, the litter swirling, the world seemingly undone.

Down the streets they hobble, their gun barrels wandering from side to side in anticipation.

"Can you hear me?" Old Burt screams.

There are dead animals lumped about their feet, and Tyler kicks at a squirrel, says, "What killed 'em?" But no one hears it, because all their ears are ringing.

Then Manny says, "La Llorona," because he sees the woman in white.

How did she move?

As a boy I had a toy soldier with a key in its back. When turned, the key wound gears. You would set the thing on a flat surface, and the unwinding of the key began—a tiny, machine noise preached from the critter—and it labored forward robotically.

This jerky, near inanimate ambulation, was akin to the woman's stroll. Clipped movements tugged her forward, and the children amassed behind her followed accordingly.

Inside the sleeping bag, Teddy tries again, "Can you hear me."

This time Scarlett answers, "Yes," then, "me?"

"Yeah," Teddy says.

"What is it?"

Teddy laughs, "I have no idea."

"Should you check?"

"I'd rather not."

Scarlett giggles. "Don't worry," she says, "I'll keep you safe."

The two are still sticky from lovemaking, but again they go at it, because they've nothing else to do.

Blue Parson pulls the last beer from the water and opens it. "What the fuck was that?" he asks.

Manny, Tyler and old Burt stand back to back to back, their guns aimed at the children whose blueness is repulsive.

"What the shit?" says Tyler. "What do we do?"

Old Burt shakes his head. "Was there something silly in that blunt?" he asks.

"Not besides weed," says Tyler.

"What'd you call her again?" says Old Burt.

"La Llorona," says Manny, "gotta be," he spits, "I always thought it was bullshit."

"What's she do again?" asks Tyler.

"Nothing, I don't think," says Manny, "just looks for her babies," he says, "dead ones."

"Well she fucking-A found 'em didn't she?" says Old Burt. Hundreds of the children wander around them, headed, seemingly, toward the bay.

Tyler sighs. "Should we shoot any of 'em?" Tyler asks.

It's quiet a bit. All that can be heard is the daffy steps of the children passing by. One of them is picking its nose. "Well they ain't really doing anything is they," says Burt, "to deserve it?"

"Nah," says Tyler, "I don't guess."

"I wanna shoot one," says Manny.

"I don't know," says Burt, "what if they retaliate."

"With what?" asks Manny. "They ain't got no weapons."

"Yeah," says Tyler, "but there's lots of 'em."

The woman in white screams again, and the three wince in pain.

"Fuck," says Old Burt, "can we shoot her?" But he's not certain if anyone can hear. She screams again and Old Burt raises his .38. He aims at her back, pulls the trigger twice. He can't hear it, but the pistol kicks twice, and two rounds plunge into her pale dress and black blood purges from the spots the shots sink, and thick rivers of the stuff drips from her, but she doesn't seem to notice.

One of the dead boys walks by Burt, and Burt places the .38 to his head, fires, and his little head explodes across the shirt of the girl walking beside him—brain grit and skull splinters—and the headless boy droops to the dirt, but the boy following him reaches down, grabs his wrist, and drags him along, the dead boy's blood leaving a trail in their wake. Other than that, they move along unbothered by it.

Burt looks at Manny, Manny looks at Tyler, they all look at each other. Burt shrugs, says, "Fuck it, they're dead anyway," and, yes, the murders ensue.

Blue takes the beer bottle back from Rob, swigs it, then looks askance. "You hear that?" Blue asks.

Rob nods. "Gunshot."

Tim says, "Too close to be hunters."

Blue says, "Too many to be hunters."

A few more shots are fired. They sound like hammers on rooftops. "That," said Rob, "was a pistol," he pauses and hears some more shots, "but there's a shotgun in there somewhere too."

"What you hunt with both?" asks Tim, who is a hunter but only casually.

Blue shakes his head, "People," he says.

Scarlett is on top of Teddy again, fucking him again, wriggling in the sex way, but she pauses. "People're shooting," she says.

"Who fucking cares?" Teddy says.

Mindy and Tessa's fear swells again when the shots start. Still coiled in each other's embrace and hunched in the road, the blue-faced children stumbling absentmindedly by them, they whimper at each other, whisper their confusion: What's happening? What is it? I don't want to open my eyes. Who's shooting? What are they? Are they gone yet? They're not gone yet? Why's this happening? When will they leave?

"One of us has to look," Mindy says.

Tessa says, "Sure as shit ain't gonna be me."

The two women have their faces hidden against the other's shoulder.

"You're such a pussy," says Mindy.

"And you?" Tessa asks.

Mindy nods, "I'm a pussy too."

It's silent a spell. Then more shots.

"Let's both look together," Mindy says.

Tessa nods her head into Mindy's shoulder. "Okay," she says.

"On three," says Mindy.

"On three," Tessa says.

"One, two, three…"

four

Old Burt, Manny and Tyler are smiling, walking weirdly through the army of children, kicking them about, firing at random. They are aloof little creatures: Old Burt sets his palm against one's forehead and the little fella just zombie-walks in place against the force of Old Burt's stiff arm. Tyler walks up, forces the barrel of his 9mm into the kid's gooey mouth, pops a round that leaps out the back of the thing's neck and zips off the concrete and catches a little brown-haired girl in the gut with a thump. The girl keeps moving, and Old Burt takes his hand off the boy's forehead, and his noggin flops to his shoulder, but on he walks.

"Manny," says Tessa, when she sees him.

"Hey," Manny says, "where'd you come from?"

Tessa points to the ground.

"Watch this," Manny says, and he puts his twelve gauge barrel against a girl's shoulder, pulls the trigger and then the girl's arm drops to the ground, followed by a belch of black blood. The girl keeps walking. Manny smiles at Tessa.

Mindy moves her way through the myriad children, makes her way to Old Burt and Tyler, "What is this?" she asks.

Old Burt shoots a few more kids, then flips open the

cylinder of his revolver, lets the empty shell casings drop to the ground, begins to reload. "Manny's got some Mexican word for it," says Old Burt, "but to me, just seems like target practice." Burt slaps the cylinder closed, shoots a few more dead kids.

Mindy flinches with each shot, hollers, "Manny?"

"Yup," Manny says. He is handing his shotgun to Tessa.

"What the hell is this?"

Tessa shoots a boy in the face, screams, "Fun as shit, is what," then, "Burt, give her your gun."

Burt shrugs, holds the butt of his .38 at her.

Mindy takes it. Shoots a kid in the throat, which blows open, bits of his larynx drape from the wound drenched in black blood that glistens in the moonlight. "I don't know," she says, "feels wrong," says Mindy as she watches the bleeding boy pass her.

Mindy hands the gun back to Burt. "Where are they going?" Mindy asks. She watches the backs of them, their creepy progression in the shadowy night, the woman in white now nearly out of view.

"Don't know," says Tyler. "Should we follow 'em?"

Old Burt says, "Might as well," then, "almost out of bullets anyhow."

The shots cease as the five walk along with the meandering children, following the woman in white as she makes her way from Scrape and out toward the bay.

Through slim fields of johnson grass and sand, they move on in the moonlight, quiet except for their walking. Their shadows hover dark beneath them.

When they reach the bay, the woman in white leads the children into the water.

The water is up to her knees. The water is up to her waist.

The water is up to her neck. The water is over her head. It doesn't take as long for the children to disappear.

"Look at this fucking mess," Blue says. He reaches down into the pile of bottles and lifts out a green one. "I ain't never had one of these," he says. He tries to twist the top off, but it won't turn. It hurts his hand. He drops it. "Some other time," he says, and he reaches for a can of Miller Lite, cracks it open, and suds foam from the mouth of it. He blows the froth to the floor, slurps his beer.

Tim is behind the counter finding cigarettes. Rob is eating chips he pilfered from a rack.

"Where's Tessa, you think?" Blue asks.

They go into the back, but it's vacant.

They return to the front of the store, eat, drink look at nudie mags, smoke, linger.

Teddy and Scarlett both cum again.

"Sh," says Scarlett. "The shots have stopped."

Teddy starts snoring.

Scarlett drops off in the music of it.

It takes half an hour for all the children to follow the woman in white out into the water. The moon shines lively on the bay, the tossing water chirping fits of light off its many crests and ebbs.

The air is salty, fresh, alive. Mindy has her shoes off, is burying her feet in the sand. Tessa is ankle-deep in the water, petting the heads of the dead children who pass her. Burt, Tyler and Manny are waiting until they can only see the backs of the children's heads to fire.

Manny keeps missing.

"That's why y'all lost the Alamo," says Old Burt.

"We didn't lose the Alamo," says Manny.

"Then why you speaking English?" asks Old Burt.

Tyler stands up. "I'm hungry," he says.

"Me too," says Mindy.

Tessa looks up. "Let's go back to the store," she says.

"Well, God damn," Tessa says when she sees Blue Parson slunk down in a pile of empty cans, dozing.

The noise wakes Blue, he shakes his head, blinks his eyes.

"Hey, hey," he says, lifts the can of High Gravity in his hand to his lips, sips at it.

"You drunk?" Tessa asks.

"Not all the way," says Blue. "But more than I ain't I guess."

Old Burt looks for a Mexican coke that's not cracked against the tiles.

Tyler has a Boone's Farm.

Manny drinks Tecate.

Mindy has a Miller.

Tim has half V8 half Budweiser.

Tessa has a Boone's Farm.

Rob Cooder eats a powdered donut. "What do you think caused it?" Rob asks, chewing as he talks, white sugar on his lips.

"Shit," says Old Burt, "you didn't see?"

"See what?" asks Blue.

"The woman," says Tessa, "the kids."

"What woman?" asks Tim, "what kids?"

"These hicks is oblivious," says Mindy, "Couldn't find

their cocks unless they caught crabs and had to scratch."

"Says you?" asks Blue, and the room goes awkward, because everyone knows.

Then Manny, "La Llorona."

"La what?" asks Rob.

"The woman," says Burt, and he eyes an undamaged Coke, plucks it from the ground and pries the top off with his lighter. The bottle bleeds suds, but he sucks them from the mouth of it, then says, "dressed in white," he takes another sip, "the thing that was screaming," he nods, "an unnatural noise."

"Yeah," says Blue, "we heard it."

"So loud, stole my ears," says Tim.

"That was it," says Tyler.

"And that wasn't all," says Old Burt, "she had all these zombie kids with her?"

"Brain eaters?" asks Blue.

"Nah," says Burt, "that was the odd thing," he laughs, "well the odd thing besides all of it," he sips his Coke again, "they didn't eat brains or nothing. Just walked out into the bay." Burt motions with his Coke bottle toward the water.

Rob Cooder finishes his donut and takes a flask from his pocket. He screws the flip lid on it, sucks a sip, offers the thing toward Burt, "Wanna spike?" he asks.

"Shit," says Burt, "I've had all the spikes I'll ever need." He pulls a chain on his neck and a medallion draws up from behind his shirt, and he lets it dangle for Cooder to see. It's a circle with a triangle in the middle.

"What's that?" asks Rob.

"AA," says Mindy. "Burt don't drink."

"Nothing harder than cola," Old Burt agrees. "Not for a dozen years."

"Shit," says Blue, "what's the point of that," and he chugs at his HG.

Old Burt nods at Blue, "I used the think the same," he says.

Then Tyler says, "Hey. Y'all seen anybody else?"

Every eye in the room looks at him.

"Huh?" asks Tessa.

"Well," says Tyler. "There's us, right, but the whole time we were shooting, didn't no one else come out their house. Seems odd."

"Shooting," says Blue, "at what?"

"The kids," says Manny.

"Why?" asks Blue, "I thought they weren't doing nothing."

Old Burt looks at Manny, and Manny looks at Tyler, and the three look at each other.

"It was complicated," says Old Burt.

"Yeah," says Manny.

"You had to be there," adds Tyler.

"We should go looking," says Mindy, then the room looks at Mindy. Mindy shakes her head, "For others, you dumb shits," and then everyone nods.

"I'm down," says Blue, "but we should take a cooler."

"Why?" asks Tessa.

"Don't know what else is out there," Blue says, "and if I gotta die, I'm dying drunk."

Most others agree with him. Only Old Burt shakes his head disapprovingly, "Rock bottom waits for all drinkers," he says.

"Don't be such a fucking buzz kill," says Mindy.

Then Tyler says, "And a hypocrite," says Tyler.

"Hypocrite?" says Old Burt. "I ain't drank in twelve years."

"No," says Tyler, "but you got blunted earlier."

Old Burt laughs. "Smoking ain't drinking," he says, "marijuana maintenance, we call it. Not everyone in the program's down, but, it's like the coins say, 'to thine own self be true.'"

"Exactly," says Blue as he puts beer in a Styrofoam cooler.

search party

We take the streets meekly.

We knock on doors that go unanswered.

Through trash swept yards, we tarry.

We seven drunkards and Old Burt shaking his head at us as we sip ourselves sillier.

Jokes are told.

Blue Parson:

A man, a woman, and a turtle go into a bar. Bartender says, "What can I get you?" Man says, a less ugly baby.

Tyler:

A fag goes to see a doctor because his dick's turned purple. Doctor says, "I've seen this condition, but not in a blue moon." The fag contemplates this, says, "Well, Doc, I guess you're cute enough. Get me some paint and bend over."

Tim:

Mom walks in on her son who's jerking off to a picture of Dick Cheney. Naturally she's disgusted. "Boy, you need help," she says. The boy looks at the picture; he looks back at his mom. "I appreciate the offer," he says, "but you're not really my type."

Mindy:

What do you call a lesbian with no tongue and no fingers? A waste of fucking time.

Tessa:

A man's on trial for rape. He tells the judge he's guilty but that the judge should be lenient on account of how small the rapist's dick is.

"The size of your dick doesn't matter," the judge says, and the rapist says, "Sorry."

"Why?" asks the judge.

"Because," the rapist says, "you'd only say that if you had a small dick too."

Old Burt:

What do you call a black guy who's never met his father? A black guy.

Rob:

What do you call a Mexican who can run fast and jump high?

Manny:

Let me guess: a wet back?

Rob:

I didn't say that Spic could swim.

In and out of cars and trucks we climb, looking for keys, but every time we find a keyed ignition, we can't get the engine to turn.

In empty homes, we lift phones from their housings, place our ears to receivers, but hear nothing emitted. No dial tones, no static.

Back in the streets, we call out names of friends and relatives:

Terry, Sally, Cindy, Tex, Guillermo, Tio, Chuy, Sebastian, Mikey, Maisy, Georgia, Molly, Andy, Sandy, Richard, Bob, Melissa, Lilly, Becky, Bailey, Victor, Jimmy, Hunter, Tom.

Nothing.

No one answers.

No one comes.

"This is creepy," says Tessa.

Above, the sky's black fades to gray, the light of coming morning, muting out the certainty of night, whispering on the paleness of day.

"I'm tired," says Blue.

"Me too," says Mindy.

"Let's go to the tree house," says Rob.

"Might be the safest place," says Old Burt, "good vantage point, I suppose. In case anything else is coming."

We all agree, and stumble to Blue's. Climb up the ladder. Pick corners to flop in. Distribute blankets we've pilfered, pillows and bedrolls.

In the dark.

In the quiet.

Our minds wander.

thoughts

MINDY

In the brightening light of Blue Parson's tree house, Mindy thinks of the semester she spent at UT Austin, living in the fourth floor of Dobie, a dorm named after a Texas legend, a man who wandered the state culling folk tales and low myths, bitter and happy stories, both, that evidenced the state's turbulent history of a place that's been fought over. She'd only read one of the things he'd written. A queer, tall tale about a man who'd used walnut husks as body armor— or so she remembered it. She'd read the thing in a library on campus, which one she couldn't remember. There were several, and they all had different names. These names were lost to her, with the exception of one—PCL. She couldn't remember the true meaning of the acronym, but, as she recalled, it was the library that housed the majority of the texts relevant to those pursuing degrees in engineering. Many of those engineering students were from Asia, so the students jokingly called it "Predominantly Chinese Library."

Mindy was at UT hoping to study nursing, but on the first floor of her dormitory was a theatre—Dobie Theatre— an independent house that showed art films, documentaries, foreign features that garnered awards, and Mindy felt called to it, spending all her money and free time there, watching stories that seemed so distant to her life's history—a bungled existence in the depressing town of Scrape, Texas.

Beyond the movies was the boy. Alexei. His neat shaved head, his precision features.

"You come here all the time," he told her.

"I like movies," she said.

"Who doesn't?" he asked.

And Mindy just shrugged.

Alexei.

Their hands touched once when he was taking her ticket.

The next time he saw her he asked, "Do you like to take walks?"

After her movie, they walked out of the theatre onto Guadalupe, the bright light of day, nearly blinding their eyes, and they held hands going south.

When they got to Cesar Chavez he led her east to Congress and south again to the bridge over Town Lake.

"You got anywhere you're supposed to be?" he asked.

"No," she told him.

Alexei looked at his watch. "In about half an hour, you're gonna see magic."

They waited. The sky grayed to dusk. Others gathered around them. Alexei said, "Don't listen to anyone," and Mindy looked at him, "to these people," he told her, "to their talking," he said, "plug your ears with your fingers. I don't want them ruining your surprise."

The sun sank behind them, orange light and murky sky.

Alexei pointed. He pulled Mindy's hands from her ears, held them, "Look, look, look, look," he said. And, to Mindy, it seemed like a cloud of smoke was wafting from the bridge beneath them, but then she realized it was something flying.

"Are they bugs?" she asked.

"Bats," he said.

Alexei.

He could make bats magic, could make bats a surprise.

Later, he bought her ice cream. Later, they were back in her dorm room.

For weeks, they wandered with each other. To the capital building made of pink granite. To the Central Market on Lamar Boulevard where Mindy stood mesmerized, staring at produce and fish. "I've never seen this kind of food," she confessed to him.

But some people's hearts need constant change to feel happy.

"You're doing what?" she asked him.

"A study," he told her.

"I don't get it."

"It's like a three week thing," he said, "I go in, take some pharmaceuticals. They monitor me. Make sure the drugs are working."

"Isn't that like, dangerous?" Mindy asked.

"Could be," he said, "but it pays good."

Alexei.

"I'll miss you," Mindy told him, the last day they saw each other.

"Don't be so dramatic," he told her.

When he was away, Mindy's symptoms showed.

Some things are nothing, but nothing can't always be forgiven.

OLD BURT

But it hadn't been a dozen years. There was a boat ride. A deep sea charter.

AA has all these acronyms.

One is HALT: hungry, angry, lonely, tired.

You don't want to be those things.

"One is too many," thought Burt, "a thousand isn't enough," he thought, "the alcoholic's mind is like a bad neighborhood, don't go there alone," thought, "this too shall pass."

Old Burt changed HALT to SHALT in his mind: the S stood for sea sick.

He was sitting there with the salt smell heavy on his breathing, the horizon bobbing up and down, a bucket of minced mullet at his feet, the sloppy sound of the waves on the hull. He knew the trick: stare at the horizon, the stillest spot on the sea, but it wasn't working. Every so often his vision chanced glances at the clouds that seemed to move in unnatural ways, and he thought he'd be puking soon, and he kept saying the serenity prayer, "God grant me . . ." But then the steward came by:

"Beers, sodas, sandwiches?" the steward asked, and Old Burt ordered three Bud Lights, chugged them like water to mask his symptoms of the churning.

It worked.

That was ten years ago.

It worked.

"To thine own self," thought Old Burt.

But sometimes truth is the last thing you need.

TYLER

Truth is, Tyler knew why he kept hanging around Old Burt: Tyler felt sorry for him.

Well, Tyler felt sorry for Burt, and he liked the old man too. He wasn't all bad. Sometimes, when it was just them, Tyler kinda thought Burt treated him like family. Shit, of all the people in the tree house, only Tyler knew.

Once, as they sat on Burt's porch drinking soda, Tyler asked him, "Why'd you quit?"

"Quit what?"

"Drinking?"

"Ah," Old Burt had told him, and Old Burt wiped beads of sweat from his glass bottle. He looked Tyler in the eye. "Used to," he said, "I had a daughter. Michelle," he said. "That was her name. Died a cancer. About eleven years back."

"Oh," said Tyler. "You quit when she died?"

"No, no," said Burt. "Before." He chuckled. "It was a promise to God." Burt looked at his shoes. "When Michelle was diagnosed, I was drinking. She and her mom had moved out the house, you see? I was always showing up messed up. Wrecking cars. Interrupting soccer practice." Old Burt shook his head. "The two girls were done with me, and they should'a been."

It was silent. Both Tyler and Burt sipped at their drinks.

"Michelle's mother called me up, Brandi," he said, "that's her name," he shook his head, "but I gotta say, I don't like saying it. But she called me up and told me she and Michelle needed to talk, and they had me drive up to Houston where they were living, took me to a Whataburger and told me the sad news over bad coffee, and I asked how I could help.

"'Burt,' Brandi told me, 'You've never been much a help at all, but we thought you should know,' and then Michelle kinda told her mother off for me, told her, 'you said you wouldn't do this,' and then her mother apologized to me, and I said that I understood.

"And, well, on the way home, it just kinda hit me. I pulled off 59 in Victoria and went down to the Riverside Park and wandered the trails there, and I came across a family picking pecans off the ground, speaking Spanish as they tucked the things into plastic bags, and then, later, I saw a herd of deer standing still off in the woods, and a hurt washed over me, but a stillness too. And I was there in the woods and a sun ray dropped down like a Jacob's Ladder, and it felt like it landed right on me, and I whispered to it, like a kid might whisper into a tin can telephone, that if God kept my daughter safe, I'd never drink again.

"I lived up to my end of the bargain, but I guess God had his fingers crossed, because I watched Michelle go skinny as a skeleton, watched all the treatments just bounce off her, maybe even make her worse, and the day she died I was holding her hand, and she said, 'don't start when I'm gone,' and I told her I wouldn't, and she said, 'and get back with Mom,' and I told her I would, and she smiled at me, and her big blue eyes dropped two tears, one from each, and she laid her head back on a pillow and the tears ran toward her ears."

Silence sat strong on the porch. No movement.

"Did ya?" asked Tyler.

"What?"

"Stay sober?"

"I did."

"And the mother."

Burt smiled. "We were together a while," he said. "Then one day I went on a fishing trip and she got mad at me. I came back, went to bed, and the next morning, when I woke up, she'd packed her things and was gone," Old Burt frowned. "She left me an e-mail address, but I've never used it. Some things are too fragile to try to put back together."

ROB

"Scrape's fucking broken."

MANNY & TESSA

"You awake?"

"Kinda."

"Think anyone else is?"

"Probably."

"I'm too tired to sleep."

"Me too," Tessa says, "isn't that funny? I've never been too hungry to eat, but when I'm beat like this, I just fidget and toss."

"I used to always have to pretend I'd been hurt."

"What?"

"I don't know," Manny says. "Like wounded or, like, sick."

Both Manny and Tessa giggle.

"Like, I'll pretend I'm an old-time soldier, been shot and in a military hospital with all kinds of dying men around me, and the smell of medicine, and people fighting to save their legs from amputation, and that I'm just there bandaged and listening to the nurse wheel carts around from bed to bed."

"You're fucking crazy," Tessa says.

"Maybe," says Manny. "But sometimes it works."

Both Manny and Tessa lie there, their minds packed with the noise imagined from military hospitals.

Manny falls asleep.

TESSA

She thinks about nurses, soldiers gut shot and bleeding.

She thinks smells—antiseptic, urine.

The noise of pain, low grunts emitting from the wounded. Whispers to gods and mothers and girlfriends.

One soldier's hand drapes from the side of his bed. From the tip of his index finger, dark blood drips into a pool on the tile floor. His hand is reflected in the pool, and each time a bead of blood increases the perimeter of the puddle, ripples distort the reflection, the blood shimmies iridescent.

There is a cart. Rusty wheels. A white clad nurse pushes it, and a sort of song emits. Her black shoes against the white tile in time, the sing song whine of rusty wheels spinning. Fluorescents flicker. A lullaby to Tessa.

And then she's asleep.

TIM

Tim's phone is near dead, but he lays beneath the covers looking at the nude pictures he's accumulated.

Some of the girls, he can't even remember their names. Girls he met at rodeos and girls he knew from high school and some women that he'd known from church and some of his mother's friends and friends' mothers and sisters of people he'd worked with.

He liked his picture collection, but it also made him feel sick.

What was wrong with him? Why was he so foul-minded?

In high school he'd had a girlfriend who'd told him he was a "good one." That's what she had said. She'd called him kind. She'd called him sweet.

She went away to school. She didn't call like she said she would.

A few Christmases later, Tim was at Rudy's, a bar that's now closed.

She was there. The girl. She had a guy with her, and the two came up to Tim, and the girl introduced Tim to the new guy by saying, "This is my friend Tim."

Friend Tim.

Friend Tim.

Tim scrolls through his pictures.

Chubby girls and black girls and white girls and girls with soft, full breasts, and girls with small tits, nipples the color of almonds.

Tim's phone says: 10% Battery.

Tim looks at a few more pictures.

Tim turns off his phone.

BLUE

Blue is drunk.
    Blue is snoring.
    Blue's too drunk to dream.
    Or too drunk to remember.
    His dreams in the morning.

MORNING

Tap.

Tap. Tap. Tap.

Tap. Tap. Tap. Tap. Tap.

"Hear that?" asks Old Burt.

"A branch?" says Blue. "The wind?"

Tap. Tap. Tap.

"Too constant," says Mindy.

They all sit up. Panic upon them.

"Someone look out the window," says Tessa.

"You look," says Blue.

"Ain't you just a fucking man," says Mindy.

"Never claimed to be," says Blue. "Ain't we in my fucking tree house?"

"I'll look," says Tyler. "Probably nothing," he says.

"After last night," says Old Burt, "it's doubtful."

Tyler goes to the window, parts the drapes, places his face to the glass.

the black,
hairy hands

Hands. Thousands, millions, scurrying on fingers like spiders or crabs. Only hands. Black, coarse hair covering them. Fingernails sharp and long. They move flicker quick over parked cars, across rooftops. They break glass, smash mailboxes, toss broken bits of Scrape to and fro, willy nilly. Pouncing on the pads of their fingers, acrobatically, unfazed, seemingly, by gravity, they cross walls un-slowed, sweeping perpendicular to the ground the way roaches or squirrels may, the tapping sound of their progression like typing or Morse code, the clickety clack of their multitudes like a million tiny locomotives chugging along miniature tracks. A static kind of hiss from their legions, a sort of white noise birthed by their oddity, and Tyler contemplates them, unaware of what to call them, but the others in the tree house sense his fear raging, sense him growing disturbed.

Some stories are so old, they split just like rivers. Headwaters birth channels that spit tributaries in all directions. The fuzzy hand, the Devil's hand, the black hand, the hand of Horta.

Some say this: it is the Spanish Inquisition and a Muslim man will not convert. Of course, this isn't exact history. He could have been a Jew, a pagan, a witch. If it is a witch it is a woman. If it is a woman, it may have been a child. Whatever it was, it stood trial for its sins against the church, was found guilty and put to death, dumped in a mass grave, and there, the magic starts. How? It is unclear. For others, it is the New World. Perhaps in modern day America. Missions are erected to convert the natives, but some refuse. Those who do are similarly sentenced to death. They are buried in indigenous graveyards where the local magic does its trick. Later still, it could be a woman who feverishly masturbates to death, the hand so intent on masturbating, that it leaves its owner who can no longer maneuver it. Or, perhaps, there is a merchant so intent on counting his jewels and coins, that his hand carries on the counting even after the merchant has passed away. In all of these myths, the result is the same: An evil hand wanders the world freely. It steals, kills and torments. It maims, interferes, harasses. In some myths, the hand can grow many times the size of a man. It carries evil children away to Satan. It kills adulterers, rapes women, steals gold.

In all of these myths, the thing is pure evil.

"I got a feeling," says Old Burt, "those things are testier than the children."

"They are," says Manny. "At least, says the legend."

"This another Mexican thing?" asks Tyler.

Manny nods, and Old Burt just stares at him. "I'm so fucking happy you fuckers lost the Alamo," he says.

Teddy rolls up the sleeping bag and Scarlett holds the pillows. She smiles at him. "You ready?" she asks.

Teddy grabs the bag, takes one last look around. "Yep," he says. He smiles back at her, "Time to hit the road." Teddy walks to the front door; Scarlett lingers behind mildly, casting a nostalgic gaze at the place they've lived the past year. She remembers the times, the day they moved in. How they'd ordered pizza and drank cheap wine from plastic cups, sitting Indian style on the floor eating, talking about how they'd decorate the place once they'd built the energy to unpack.

The door opens.

Scarlett hears it.

Hears Teddy step into the day.

But then, another sound . . .

"How many rounds y'all got left?" Old Burt asks Manny and Tyler.

The boys fish their pockets, check their clips, look at Burt with worry. "Four bullets," says Tyler, and Manny says, "Six shells."

"I got four rounds in my revolver," he looks out the window. "Eighteen shots total," he continues, then beneath his breath begins fruitlessly counting the many queer creatures. "We are surely fucked," he says.

Teddy screams, "Close the door," and Scarlett turns to the sound of his screaming.

From inside the dark room, outdoors shines devastatingly bright, hideously lit, so the shape of the door seems the sharpest rectangle ever laid eyes on by man. In that rectangle, Scarlett sees, though she can't quite comprehend it, the black, hairy hands converging on Teddy, fits of them creeping up his legs and torso, and Teddy punching them from him, but there are way too many.

If she were closer, she would see, the evil hands clenched tight to Teddy's clothes, plucking his balance from him as the weight of the hands slowly but surely drags him down to the cement, where the critters clutch him to the ground and begin to scrape into his flesh, working their way into his muscles, spilling his blood, as Teddy screams his anguish, launches his imperative again at Scarlett, "Close the door, close the door, close the door." And she flings herself to the knob of the thing, slams it shut, falls to her knees against it hysterically, sobbing a terror-laden woe.

Outside Teddy's eyes are open toward the bluest sky he'll ever see, and the fingers of the hands are moving lickety split, mincing his body into bits, flecks and globules—

Teddy's blood draining out across the white cement of the driveway all around them.

Blue Parson's opens a beer, guzzles it.

"How many of those are left?" Old Burt asks.

Blue lowers his beer from his lips, pants breath, wipes his mouth with the back of a hand. "Thought you didn't drink," he says.

"I don't," says Old Burt, "but just fucking tell me."

Blue looks into the ice chest. "Four Millers," he says, "one Bud."

"All cans?" Old Burt asks.

Blue nods, "All cans," he says.

"Burt, what the hell you getting at?" asks Mindy.

Old Burt looks at her. "Well," he says, "there's five us guys," he looks at each of the men, "and, if it comes to it, one of us might need to create a distraction," he looks out the window at the hands, "I'm not certain they know we're here, or what their intentions are, but, when they figure it out, and we figure them out, one of us might need to draw 'em off." He looks at Tessa, looks at Mindy. "I wouldn't feel right asking one of you ladies to do it," he smiles, "might mean certain death and all," he says. He looks out the window again. "We ain't got no straws," he says, "I'm proposing we pluck beers for it. Reach in blind, each of us men," he nods at the others, "whoever gets the Bud, gets the duty."

"Wait, wait, wait," says Tim. "There's six guys. Me, Blue, you, Manny, Tyler and Rob."

Old Burt laughs. "I would never trust this job to no nigger," he says, and Tyler is almost certain Old Burt winks at him.

Blue finishes his beer, drops it on the ground and steps on it. "Let's do it," he says, "so we can get back to drinking 'em."

Tyler pulls a Miller.

Blue pulls a Miller.

Old Burt pulls the Bud. He smiles. "Figures," he says, "beer's been an eternal enemy."

drawing
them off

Old Burt takes Manny's shotgun, gives it to Tyler, takes Tyler's pistol. "Shotgun's the best weapon to protect against intruders," he says to Tyler, "and Manny can't shoot for shit."

"What are you gonna do?" asks Tessa.

Old Burt looks at her, "I got an arsenal in my house," he says, "automatic rifles, grenades, a flame thrower." He nods, "I'm gonna try to get over there, make massacre on these little nigger hands." Then Old Burt opens his Bud. "Bill W. asked for whiskey on his death bed," Old Burt says, "he was the founder of AA," he sips the beer, "nurses refused him, said he was out of his wits with the pain, said he would regret it. I'm not certain how. He died a day or so later. You think God gets mad at you for falling off the wagon right before you die?" Old Burt asks.

Blue opens another beer, "Who gives a shit?" he says, and Old Burt and Blue cheers.

Below the tree house, the hands are growing thicker, festering like a business of flies, climbing each other, knocking each other down.

"They know," says Old Burt. "It's time," he chambers a round in the 9 mm, tucks the gun in his waist band. "The zip line will hold me?"

"Tested at over 300 pounds," Blue says.

"I'm well under that," says Old Burt.

"This is crazy," says Tessa.

"What part of it?" asks Rob.

Old Burt zips out into the air above the black hands. They seem aware of him, follow him down the line.

He lands in a clearing, draws the 9mm and blasts two rounds, runs toward his house.

The hands give chase, begin to circle him in the road. He fires two more rounds, then throws the unloaded 9, draws his .38.

He jumps over a progression of hands, shoots once and a hand explodes, its fingers toss in several directions. He kicks a few away from him, runs on, fires another shot.

There is a stalled F-150, and Old Burt jumps on the hood of it, climbs to the cabin roof, surveys the hands surrounding him.

He reaches his free hand in his pocket, pulls out a Miller. He cracks it open, begins chugging away.

Several of the hands have reached his legs. He kicks again, fires again. The beer is empty. He flings the empty can down at the hands. He places the mouth of his .38 to the side of his head. He waves goodbye toward the tree house. Old Burt cocks back the hammer. Old Burt squeezes the trigger.

His brains are forced out his skull in a gush, and the hands climb upon him, begin to scrape him apart.

"Know why he drank Coke so much?" asks Tyler.

Everyone in the tree house is silent.

"He said it was the most racist drink he knew. He said that used to, years and years ago, it was made from wine and cocaine and sold as a sex drink, and that lots of people in Europe loved it. He told me the Pope drank the stuff, and gave the inventor a medal for it. He said that, when Coke finally got to the states, that they had to take the wine out because of some temperance movement, but that, for a long time, they'd left the cocaine in. He said that at first, they only sold the stuff in drug stores that black folks couldn't go to on account of Jim Crowe laws, but, when they figured out how to bottle it, that black folks could drink it, and white folks had this idea that blacks were drinking the stuff and running around raping white women, so they decided to take the cocaine out to stop all the raping."

It is quiet again.

Then Tessa asks, "Tell me again why the hell you hung out with him?"

Tyler doesn't answer her.

"What now?" says Mindy when the black hands head back toward the tree house.

"I've got three shells," says Tyler. "Anyone want me to shoot 'em?" They look at him nervously. "In the head," Tyler clarifies. "You won't feel anything." Tyler looks out the window. "It's either that or them," he says. "I'll probably do myself, once they get closer."

Rob says, "Yeah, do me." He steps forward, and Tyler puts the barrel of the 12 gauge against it.

"You sure?" Tyler asks.

And then they hear the bell ringing.

ding dong

We hear four low drones, and the hands seem called to attention, seem beckoned elsewhere, and they go.

Reluctantly, it seems, based on the speed of their movements, they drag along on the tips of their fingers toward the ringing, away from Scrape.

"What is it?" asks Blue.

"Couldn't tell you," says Manny.

Silence for a moment, but then the bell chimes again.

A pleasant sound.

Sort of peaceful.

"Is it all over?" asks Mindy, and then we hear the whip.

Out the window of the tree house, we see, walking toward us, a bull whip in his hand, horns on his head, his face masked by a flour tortilla, dressed in black, some wicked, aged creature who calls out, "Have these children been good?"

Tyler looks at Manny, "What is it?" he asks.

"El Abuelo," Manny answers, "The Grandfather."

"What does he do?" says Blue.

"Asks us questions," Manny answers.

Tyler motions with the shotgun, "Well," he says, "let's go answer him."

Tyler, Manny, Mindy, Rob, Blue, Tessa and Tim climb down from the tree house, stand shoulder to shoulder, three on each side of Tyler who aims the gun at El Abuelo.

"Well?" El Abuelo says, "have these children been good?" His voice is old and gravelly.

Tyler says, "What the fuck you talking about?" and El Abuelo's tortilla face shows anger.

"Curses?" he asks, and he cracks his whip and Tyler's cheek splits open, bloody, and Tyler fires two shells at El Abuelo, but the birdshot only sinks into his black-leather shirt, does not faze him. El Abuelo cracks his whip again, and it wraps around the barrel of the shotgun, and he pulls back, and the gun flies to rest at El Abuelo's feet.

The seven are terrified.

"You," says El Abuelo, pointing at Blue, "Recite the catechism."

"What?" says Blue, and El Abuelo cracks his whip again at Blue, and Blue's body bursts into a puff of smoke that floats away on the breeze.

"You?" El Abuelo says, pointing to Tessa who only hides her face with her hand, and she is also whipped into smoke. Tim, the same. Rob, the same. Tyler says, "Fuck you." Mindy says, "I'll suck your dick." And they are all smoke. All but Manny. "You, my child?" El Abuelo says, "Recite."

Manny says, "Oh my God, I am heartily sorry for having offended thee and I detest all my sins, because I dread the loss of heaven and the pains of hell, but most of all because they offend thee, my God, who are all good and deserving of all my love. I firmly resolve, with the help of thy grace, to confess my sins, to do penance, and to amend my life."

El Abuelo puts his whip away. He takes Manny by the hand. The two leave Scrape forever.

the devil

A white owl circles above Scrape.

It is the only living thing in sight.

It turns left endlessly, gliding a certain course above the damage below.

Scattered glass and lumps of deadness.

Cracked cement and busted cars.

Below, Teddy's blood glistens on his skeleton.

The owl's path aims for that spot, landing on Teddy's busted open chest, where it begins to pick at the meat the hands left behind.

The door to Teddy and Scarlett's garage apartment opens.

The white owl takes notice.

The door to Teddy and Scarlett's garage apartment closes.

The white owl dips its beak back at Teddy's carnage again, raises its face, bloodstained.

The white owl chews.

The white owl swallows.

"Who do you think I am?" he asks her.

"I don't know," she says.

"That's a pity," he says. "I know you. I've watched you many times, Scarlett. With him," he points toward the door, "with others, alone."

Scarlett shakes her head, frowns at him.

"C'mon," he says. "Take a guess."

She stares at his suit, shiny red, his blue eyes and pale hair. "I'd say," she says, "you're no good," she tells him.

He smiles. "You couldn't be more correct." He nods at her. "Take off your clothes."

She doesn't know why, but she does. She unbuttons her blouse, unhooks her bra. She is terrified but she is wet, anticipating. She brings a breast to her face, licks the nipple, suckles.

He smiles.

She unbuttons her jeans, plunges her hand into her crotch, her wetness.

He moves toward her, and she pulls her underwear down. He puts his hand on her face. "You have no idea," he tells her. "You have no idea."

dissolve

Broken glass.
    Spilled blood.
    Scrape, Texas.

TOM WILLIAMS

Tom Williams is the author of one novel, *Don't Start Me Talkin*, and *The Mimic's Own Voice*, a novella. He chairs the English Department at Morehead State University.

BRIAN ALLEN CARR

Brian Allen Carr lives in the Rio Grande Valley of Texas. His short fiction has appeared in *Ninth Letter, Boulevard, McSweeney's Small Chair, Hobart* and other publications. His books include *Motherfucking Sharks* (Lazy Fascist Press), *Short Bus* (Texas Review Press), *Edie and the Low-Hung Hands* (Small Doggies Press), and *Vampire Conditions* (Holler Presents).

CPSIA information can be obtained
at www.ICGtesting.com
Printed in the USA
LVHW091549160220
647097LV00004B/749